DATE DUE		
SEP 1 2 1981		
JUN 4 1985		
OCT 2 9 1985		
MAR 8 1989		
MAY 2 3 1989		
MAY 7 1990		
JUN 1 1 1991		
NOV 3 1992		

Crazy in Love

Crazy in Love

by Richard Kennedy

illustrated by Marcia Sewall

A Unicorn Book
E. P. Dutton • New York

Library of Congress Cataloging in Publication Data

Kennedy, Richard, date   Crazy in love.

(A Unicorn book)
SUMMARY: Only recently married, a young man and woman
each begin to fear, with fairly good cause, that the other is crazy.
I. Sewall, Marcia. II. Title.
PZ7.K385Cr 1980 [Fic] 80-189 ISBN: 0-525-28364-1

Published in the United States by E. P. Dutton, a Division
of Elsevier-Dutton Publishing Company, Inc., New York

Published simultaneously in Canada by Clarke,
Irwin & Company Limited, Toronto and Vancouver

Editor: Emilie McLeod   Designer: Emily Sper

Printed in the U.S.A. First Edition
10 9 8 7 6 5 4 3 2 1

for Emilie McLeod
in person

There was a young woman who lived alone on a small farm far in the country. She worked alone, and ate alone, and sighed alone, and slept alone, and cried alone. And when she laughed, which was not often, she laughed alone. Her name was Diana.

Now one beautiful spring day she was working in the garden. With her head down, she chopped at the earth with her hoe. The sweet breeze blew her long hair across her face. Several times she brushed it back over her shoulders, but at last she threw down the hoe and said aloud, "Oh, this is impossible!"

The work was not that hard, but the spring breeze and the singing of the woodland birds and the gentle warmth of the sun were difficult to bear. She wanted to turn to someone and say "Here, see!" and "There, listen!" and "Touch this!" And she wanted just to look at someone and share the spring day. She was young, and she was tired of being alone. Arching her back in a stretch, she looked down the narrow roadway that passed her place. But rarely did anyone come down that roadway. Rarely did Diana go up that roadway to town. There were goats to milk every twelve hours. Sighing deeply, she gave the hoe a feeble kick.

Diana reached in her pocket then for a piece of string, and she was tying back her hair when she heard a birdcall that pleased her especially. She walked out of the garden toward the sound and into the woods. When the bird called again, she followed the sound. "Not a phoebe," she said to herself. "No, and not a vireo." She stepped lightly now, hoping to catch a glimpse of the bird. It called again, and she followed. "Nor a hermit thrush, either," she mused, and she followed.

In a short while, Diana found herself in a part of the woods that was strange to her. She had not spied the bird she sought, which now had stopped singing. "Ah, too bad," she said, and turned back on her way. But then she heard a singing again. Only this time it was not the song of a bird. It was a woman's voice, farther off in those unknown woods. But no one lives over that way, Diana thought to herself. The brush was thicker there, and she had to part it with a stick as she moved toward the voice, which continued singing. The more clearly she heard it, the sweeter it was; but the song was a slow and sad song, nearly like a wail or a lament.

In another few minutes Diana parted her way through some heavy bushes, and at once she was standing on the edge of a small glade which was nearly in the shape of a circle. Wild flowers were dotted about the edges of the glade, and the grass within looked almost cared for by a gardener, so nicely was it cropped by deer. A fresh breeze blew across the small meadow, and several birds sang in the near woods. And there, in the middle of the glade, bathed in the gentle sunshine, was an old broken-down shack. From out of the shack, very distinctly now, came the voice of a woman, high and sad and lonely, singing her song.

Diana walked across the grass, slightly bent forward and hesitant, for she had a notion she might be trespassing. She walked right up to the shack. Some boards were loose. Diana set her feet carefully and peered between two of the boards to see who the strange singer was in this peculiar place. Immediately as she looked in, she raised her hand to her mouth to silence her gasp of astonishment and distress. For there in the little shack was a beautiful woman in a white robe who was chained to a great millstone. She

was singing her sad song as she pushed the great stone around and around.

Diana could not keep her voice in. "Oh!" she cried, and leaped to the door of the shack, pushed it open and ran to the beautiful chained woman. "Oh," Diana cried again, "who has done this to you? What cruelty has been done here, what monster has chained you to this stone? Oh, let me break these chains, let me find a tool to set you free." And she began searching the small shack for a piece of iron to break the chains. The beautiful woman stopped pushing the millstone. She looked with tenderness and sympathy upon Diana. Then she spoke.

"Nay, do not rush about so, for you cannot release me from these chains. This is no cruelty, and no monster has me imprisoned here. This that I do, and that I am here, is an enchantment, and only a certain passing of time can set me free. Come, talk to me as I go around."

Diana was not much calmed by this gentle

and patient answer. She came to the beautiful woman and covered her hands with her own, and helped her push. "Oh, dear!" said Diana. "This is terrible! Surely something can be done."

"Nothing for me this moment," said the woman. "But I can do something for you. I can grant your wish."

"My wish? I have no wish but to set you free."

"You must think," said the woman, "for there is another wish you have. I know this, because no one may find me here except that they have a wish very dear to them. No one may hear my song unless they have a deep longing. So think carefully now. What is it you wish for?"

Diana walked around slowly with the chained woman, and she remembered that surely she did have a wish most close to her heart. And she blushed.

"Ah," said the beautiful woman, noticing.

"All right, then," said Diana, throwing her

7

head back. "Don't you know? I wish I had a husband, and that he loved me and that I loved him, and that we could share our lives together."

"Then you shall have a husband," said the woman. "Your wish is granted. But you must do something for me in return."

"Oh, I will very gladly, and for nothing except to make this hard task easier for you."

"I know that, my dear, but nevertheless you shall have a husband, and this is what I ask in return." The beautiful woman then bent her head toward her closely chained hands and said, "There, you see? I haven't even the freedom to brush my hair with my fingers. Day after day with the dust and the sweat and the falling about my shoulders it has become terribly tangled and stringy and knotted. Once it was beautiful, and I hate that I cannot care for it properly."

Diana immediately put her hands up and began unsnarling the chained woman's long hair.

"Thank you, dear, but you must bring a

8

brush, and you must walk around with me and brush my hair and talk with me, for I am lonesome. Will you do this to get a husband?"

"I would do it anyway."

"But when you have a husband, then you *must* do it. That must be your promise. Every day you must come here alone to walk with me for one hour and brush my hair, to be a comfort and company to me. That is what I ask."

"That is no hard promise," said Diana, "and I promise it with gladness."

The woman smiled and spoke for the last time. "Leave now. And when you have a husband, remember me. Take your hairbrush from home and come to me. This is your promise. Now, farewell."

Immediately the beautiful woman began singing again. Diana walked to the door of the shack, said "Farewell," and strode out across the glade, into the forest, and home.

Now all this happened early in the day, and

Diana was making a fire for the midday meal when she heard a call from outside the house.

"Hey! Cut and stack some wood for a dinner?"

She looked out the window. There stood a young man, a woodcutter, with a bucksaw over his shoulder and an axe in his hand.

"You could split some wood!" she yelled back at him. "Right there!" She pointed to a pile of wood.

The young man twirled the saw off his shoulder, spit on his hands, and walked up to the splitting block with a professional eye on the stack of wood. "I can do that little bit before you can boil a potato." He smiled at Diana, kicked a round of wood from the stack, set it on the splitting block, and turning to Diana again said, "Ready . . . Go!" Then he slung into his work. Diana opened her mouth, closed it, and ran to get a potato.

They also had a salad, warmed-up roast

chicken, some peach preserves, and at last were enjoying their coffee. The young man took out his pipe and said, "Do you mind?" Diana shook her head. He filled the pipe with tobacco and punched it down with his thumb. Then lit up. He glanced around, then stuck the burned match behind his ear. So, sitting comfortably at the table by the window that looked towards the woods, they talked.

It was Diana who talked mostly, and although she was a bit past her good manners for the many questions she asked, it could be understood. She had so little company. The woodcutter himself seemed not to mind, and he answered openly and in good humor.

"Then you have no home?" Diana asked for the second time.

"Only where I lay my back at night," said the young man. He took a deep puff at his pipe. "But it's a good life. I go where I wish. I have my axe and my saw, I have my work. That's home to me." He studied his pipe and then added, as if woodcutting were a highly appointed office: "But that sort of life isn't for everyone of course. There's many couldn't do it."

Diana nodded and waited for him to go on.

"Oh, yes, there's hardship sometimes. There's a lot to say for carrying your home around with you and eating on the way, only you've got to be lucky sometimes or you *don't* eat. Here's an example right now. I was lucky your man wasn't here when I happened by, or else he'd not let me split that wood for dinner and I'd have to go on and be hungry."

"That wasn't lucky," said Diana. "I just have no man."

The young man looked at his pipe again, and cleared his throat. He looked up. "Ah . . . my name is Dan," he said.

"My name is Diana."

They both looked down. Dan started to tap
the bowl of his pipe on his boot. He glanced
up. Diana nodded.

"You know," he said, knocking the pipe and
sticking it back in his pocket, "that was a fine
dinner. I don't know when I've had such a good
dinner lately."

"But I didn't even reckon on having a guest."

"That don't matter about how good it was,"
said Dan.

"The chicken was a bit dry, being leftovers."

"I hardly noticed."

"Just barely," said Diana. "I just barely noticed."

"In fact," said Dan, "I didn't notice at all."

"Well," said Diana, "neither did I."

They smiled at each other, then for a moment were silent. Dan tapped a finger on the table and looked around the floor.

"I admire the way you stacked that wood," Diana said.

"You do?"

"Sometimes it falls over when I stack it."

"Well, I was hungry, you know, and hurrying a little, but I can stack it better than that. You noticed how that west corner is a little crooked?"

"I just hardly noticed at all."

"Not much, just barely. I barely noticed it myself."

"In fact," said Diana, "I didn't notice it at all."

"Come to think of it," said Dan, "neither did I."

Again they smiled, and again they fell silent. Dan jumped in his seat when Diana spoke to him next.

"What are you looking around the floor for?"

"Ma'am," said Dan. "I mean Diana. I'd sure like to do some more work for you instead of going right on down the road. I could split and stack enough wood for a week before suppertime, if you'd be kind enough to share your table with me again."

Diana closed her eyes and touched her lips with her fingers thoughtfully. "That shoat pig is ready for butchering," she said, and opened her eyes and looked brightly at him. "Have you ever ate roast suckling pig with cranberry glaze?"

"Ohhhh, ma'am," Dan said, slapping his belly with both hands and pushing his chair back. "I mean Diana. I just got to get at that wood."

So they both went about their work, and whenever he came up with wood from the forest, she was near the window and would wave out at him. And he would wave back and sometimes let out a yell and go galloping off into the woods again like a clown; and she laughed, and he turned and laughed back.

The day passed wonderfully for both in their work. The wood, enough for a week, was stacked beautifully, and the roast suckling pig with cranberry glaze was delicious. And any two people would have said so, even if they weren't falling in love. Dan lit his pipe over coffee when they had finished with the strawberry shortcake, and she pushed the lid of a jar toward him. He dropped the match in it and smiled, then let out a sigh.

"Tired?" Diana asked.

"Tired? No." He drew on his pipe. "Just thinking."

"Just thinking?" she said.

"About wood," said Dan.

"About wood?"

"About how I spend most of my day cutting wood for people, and how I never really get to see the best part of it."

"How do you mean that?"

"I mean when I leave. I mean when I go along the road and it's getting dark, or when I'm sleeping in a field, and I watch the smoke come out of a chimney, and the little sparks. I know it's wood I cut there in the fireplace that's doing it, and the people are sitting around and talking, or maybe just being quiet and watching into the fire, being together." Dan took a puff on his pipe. "But I never get to see that part of it. I don't have any times like that."

"It is beautiful," said Diana. "But if you're alone you don't often do that either, just sit by the fire and watch. It's something that almost needs two people to enjoy for as much as it's worth."

"That's my thinking," said Dan.

There wasn't anything more said for a long while, and a slight chill came into the house as the stove fire burned down. They found themselves staring into the dark fireplace, and in the same moment looked at each other.

"I could start a fire in the fireplace," Diana said quietly.

And just as quietly, Dan said, "I could get some good heartwood from outside."

So in a short while they were sitting before a fine fire, and they talked together and dreamed at it until it was late and time for bed. Dan said he'd be much obliged to sleep in the barn, but Diana said he could sleep on the floor, and she doubled up the rug for a mattress and brought him a quilt. She knelt on the floor to smooth out his bedding. He knelt across from her and helped. His hands touched hers. Then they were holding hands and looking at each other. And then they were kissing.

The smell of bacon and eggs woke Dan. He jammed his legs into his trousers, looped into his suspenders, and clomped to the kitchen table in his untied boots. Diana turned from the stove and watched him tie his boots.

"Coffee?" Diana said.

"Lovely," Dan said.

They ate breakfast one-handed, for they were holding hands with the other, except when they buttered the toast. Dan finished and said, "You are the best cook in the whole world."

"And you're the best woodcutter," Diana said.

"Yesterday was nothing," Dan said. "Yesterday I was only *half* alive. You watch me cut wood today." He stood up.

"Not right now," Diana said. "Later. Right now let's go to town and get married."

Dan took her hand. She stood up and he put his arms around her waist, and she, her arms around his neck. "Right now let's do that," said Dan. And they kissed awhile, tasting like bacon and eggs and buttered toast and other good things.

And they did that. They went to town and got married. They walked all about the town after that, looking at the houses and the bridges and the churches and the people working and in shops. Then they listened to a small street band and watched a goat who appeared to be dancing. Very often they laughed, and less often they were so quiet and serious and so far away in their eyes that you might have thought they'd never find their way back. But a child playing across their path or a chasing dog would bring them back with a laugh. Everyone could see that they were in love.

They stayed that night in a small inn. The innkeeper's and his wife's eyes twinkled at them. The wife said to them that it was a nice room, and the innkeeper said it was a nice bed. After they had left, Diana stared out of the window, while Dan stared at a picture on the wall. Neither of them had the slightest idea what they were seeing. Then Dan and Diana went to bed on their wedding night.

Now the next day, when they had returned to their small place in the country, they had just finished the midday dinner when Diana got up and took her hairbrush from the dresser.

"I think I'll go for a walk in the woods," she said.

She remembered her promise to the chained lady with the tangled hair. She would go out now and brush her hair and walk with her for an hour, and talk with her, to keep her promise, because her wish for a husband had been granted.

"Good," said Dan. "I'll finish this pipe and we'll go together."

"No, dear, I believe I'll go alone."

"Oh?" Dan said, and looked at her for a few moments. "Well . . . all right." He watched her go out the door, then watched her from the window as she walked into the woods, hairbrush in hand. "Huh!" he grunted, and got himself another cup of coffee.

Diana found the small fresh glade without much trouble, for again the singing led her. She entered the door with joy and her heart full of talk to share with the beautiful woman. Together they walked around, the chained woman pushing the heavy millstone and Diana unsnarling and brushing her long hair.

"And is he handsome?" asked the lady.

"More handsome than I can tell you, although most people would hardly notice it. And strong,

and tender, and who would believe such rough
hands could touch so softly?"

"Tell me about the town, then. What did you
see, where did you go?"

Diana told everything she could think of, and
very shortly, so it seemed to them both, the hour
was up and they parted. "Again tomorrow," said
the enchanted lady.

"Again tomorrow," said Diana happily.

"There is much more to tell you. Oh, it's wonderful."

"Then tomorrow."

"Then," said Diana. She left, and hurried across the glade and into the forest.

When she returned to the house, Dan asked her if she had enjoyed her walk in the woods. She said she had enjoyed it very much, and Dan said, "Hmmmmmm . . ."

Then it was evening. Then it was night. Then it was morning the next day, then the sun was high, and then they ate. After eating, Diana took up her hairbrush and said, "I believe I'll go for a walk in the woods."

"I'll go, too," said Dan, knocking his pipe out on his boot.

"No," Diana said, touching his shoulder. He sat down again. "I'll go alone. I enjoy a walk alone."

"Hmmmm," Dan said. "Well . . ."

She was gone out the door. Dan watched her

from the window as she entered the forest. He rubbed his chin and again said, "Hmmmm."

"He is *so* wonderful," Diana said to the chained lady. "And funny, too. Let me tell you what he did last night." So they talked and walked around together. Diana brushed her companion's hair and they smiled and laughed. Near the end of the hour, Diana was quiet for a time. Then she asked, "How did you come to be chained up like this? Because it does seem a cruel thing, this enchantment."

"No, not cruel," said the lady. "Haven't you guessed? This is a punishment, and something I have deserved."

"A punishment? Then for what, dear lady? Oh, I shouldn't ask that. Forgive me."

"Don't be troubled," said the woman. "In time the enchantment will wear off, and I am happy to tell you how it came about, since it is a lesson. You see, I was once one of those people who do not believe in enchantments. And because of that, I must suffer to be enchanted myself, and to be chained and push this millstone around."

"Oh, how unfortunate," said Diana. And she meant how unfortunate that the woman had never believed in enchantments, for Diana never had any doubts about enchantments. "And how long must this be? Not that I regret that I must come and visit with you, but I ask only for your sake. How soon will you be free?"

"There is no knowing that," said the woman. "But one day you will come to me and you won't find me here. That will mean that I am free and that you are free of your promise, and I will never be here again."

This visit ended in silence and sadness. And as Diana entered the forest to go home, she listened to the enchanted lady's lonely singing, and she wept.

"Have you been crying?" Dan asked when she came in.

"Only a very little," Diana said. She smiled at him. "But I am very happy."

Dan could not understand this at all. He felt awkward around his wife that evening. It seemed he could not find the right things to say, and he watched her and wondered what was troubling her.

The next day at the regular time, Diana said that she was going for a walk in the woods.

"Good," Dan said, stuffing his pipe. He didn't look up.

She paused at the door and looked at him over her shoulder. "Wouldn't you want to go with me?" she asked, even though she would not have allowed it.

"No," said Dan. "I'll do a little work in the garden."

"Hmmmm," she said, and out she went, looking back once more before she entered the forest.

Then Dan was immediately up and out of his

chair. He stuck his hat on, watched the woods for a minute, then ran to where his wife had disappeared. He was going to find out where she walked all alone. And he worried about her crying. There was now the very rough beginning of a path where his wife had trod on her errand, and he followed it slowly, careful not to come too close to the sound of his Diana whisking through the brush up ahead of him.

Presently he heard a donkey bray. It was off in the direction he was following. He crouched low, parted the bushes carefully, and he almost stumbled into the glade when he came upon it. But he pulled back behind a bush and looked. There in the center of the small glade was an old shack, and he could hear his wife's voice inside it. She seemed to be talking to someone. Now what could all this be? he wondered. He left the bush on his hands and knees and crawled across the grass until he was right up against the shack and looking through a broken board.

And there inside was his wife, walking around and around with an old donkey that was pushing a millstone, and she was brushing the old donkey's mane and talking to it, telling the animal all about the time of the day past, and about himself.

Dan was stunned. He fell back sitting on the grass. Dragging himself across the glade into the hiding bushes, he crept in and leaned on a tree. "Oh, oh!" he said aloud. "Oh, my poor wife is crazy! My poor wife is completely mad. Oh, I have married a poor crazy wife!"

The thought of it fairly scattered his senses, and he wandered off towards home. "Oh! Each day she goes out and combs a donkey's mane and talks to it like it was a person. How long has this been going on? What can I do?"

Dan had never known a crazy person, and he didn't at all know what was best to do or say, and he was very confused. Therefore he got lost on the way home, but he found a stream that led

back. He sat for a while on the bank, resting. He held his head in his hands and rocked and moaned for his poor crazy wife. Then he heard a voice call out to him.

"Hey, youngster, you got any tobacco?"

Dan looked up. There was no one else on the stream bank. The voice called again.

"Over here! You got any tobacco? I sure could use a smoke."

And there! There in the middle of the stream, sitting on a mound of sticks, was an old man with a white beard, dressed in overalls. Dan stared for a moment, then said, "Yeah, I've got some tobacco. What are you doing out there? If you want a smoke, swim on in."

"Can't," said the old man. "I'm enchanted, and I got to sit out here on these sticks till it wears off. Sure do miss my tobacco. Would you mind swimming out here so an old man could have a smoke?"

"Enchanted?"

"You got it. Enchanted right down to my toes. Now hold that tobacco over your head so it don't get wet, mind."

Dan studied the distance across the water. The stream wasn't swift, and possibly he could wade out to the old man.

"Hold on there, grandfather," he said, then took out his pipe, matches, and tobacco. Carefully, he stepped into the water. It came up to his knees, then to his waist, then up to his chest, but his footing was solid. Only for the last couple of yards did Dan have to paddle with one arm, all the while holding the tobacco safe in the air in his free hand.

"Easy there, son," the old man cautioned. He gripped Dan's arm when he was near enough and pulled him up onto the pile of sticks. And there they sat.

Dan handed the tobacco and pipe to the old

man, who made up a smoke while Dan squeezed his wet clothes. He studied the old man while he lit up and took a great draw on the pipe.

"Ahhhhhh . . ." said the old man.

"Did you say *enchanted*?" Dan asked.

"Um." The old man took another draw on the pipe and passed it to Dan. "Yep. Just as soon not talk about it. But that's my problem." He tapped his fingers and looked at the pipe. Dan took a smoke and handed it back. "And what's your problem, son? I seen you sitting over there with a burden on your mind so heavy I almost hated to call out, but you know how it is with smoking if you got the habit. What's your grief, son?" He smoked and watched Dan.

Dan put his head in his hands again. "It's my wife," he said.

"Uh-huh," said the old man. "Woman trouble. Might have known it. Well, I can give you a wish, if you think maybe that'd help."

"A wish?"

"Sure. Nobody sees me out here unless they need a wish, so I guess you need one. Couple of years ago some fellow was fishing that little falls up there above us. Smoking a pipe, too. Fished all day and smoked all day. It about drove me crazy, that smoke drifting down here. I shouted at him for hours, promised him all sorts of stuff, but he didn't notice at all. See—he didn't need a wish, so he didn't see me or hear me." The old man took a long draw off the pipe and passed it back to Dan. "So what's wrong about your wife? You can make a wish for it to be different. She getting fat, ugly, ornery, skinny?"

"She's . . . crazy."

The old man was silent for a while. Then he said, "If you ain't going to smoke any, pass that pipe back." Dan did. "Crazy, huh? Well, I known some crazy people in my time. What's it like with your wife?"

"Every day," Dan began and he sniffed and wiped his eyes. "Every day, grandfather, she goes

off into the woods to an old mill. She goes in there, where there's an old donkey, and she brushes its mane and walks around with it and talks to it like it was a real person."

The old man nodded and spit in the water. "Well, there's worse things can happen with a woman than taking up with a donkey. Might be best just to let it be." The old man let this meditation sink in, then he spoke again. "But if you really want it so she doesn't go off visiting donkeys anymore, you can take a wish on it and that's the way it'll be."

"You can do this? You can give me a wish?"

"Yep, just like I said. You get a wish, and if you like her better not crazy, that's how you'll have her."

"Then I wish it," Dan said.

"Then that's it," said the old man. "But you got to do something for me, you know."

Dan nodded eagerly. "Anything, grandfather."

"Each day you got to come out here and smoke with me, and keep me company for about an hour. That all right with you?"

"And then my wife won't be crazy anymore?"

"In a little while. You got to watch for it. Generally shows up in the eyes. You'll know when she's all right. And when she is, then you don't have to come out here anymore." The old man took one last long draw at the pipe and gave it back to Dan. "You go now, and I'll see you tomorrow."

"But can I believe you?" Dan said. "I mean, this talk about enchantments and wishes . . ."

The old man sighed and looked up and down the stream. "I'd advise you to believe it," he said. "Go on now." He pushed Dan off his seat. "Just remember to come back tomorrow about this time. Your wife will be all right."

Dan entered the water with pipe, matches and tobacco held over his head. When he reached the shore he turned and waved.

"Just don't forget the tobacco," said the old man.

Dan followed the stream and found his way home by an easy route, which he would re-member for the next day's visit with the old man. Diana was already in the house when he arrived.

"How did you get so wet?" she asked.

"Oh . . . I fell in the stream."

"That was careless," she said.

The next day, after finishing the midday dinner, Diana took up her brush and announced that she would go for a walk in the woods. Dan said that was fine, and he poured another cup of coffee.

"Are you feeling all right?" Diana asked him.

"Fine," said Dan, and he settled himself at the table.

She went out. Dan watched her go towards the woods. A couple of times she looked back, and Dan pulled his head out of sight so she would not see him watching her.

A minute after she entered the woods, he stuck his hat on, patted his shirt pocket to make sure he had his pipe and tobacco, then went out the back door and down to the stream. He easily found his way downstream to where the old man was sitting on the pile of sticks, exactly the same as the day before.

"Hey!" yelled the old man. "I been thinking about you all morning. I mean I been thinking about smoking, but you're all right, too. Now don't get that tobacco wet, son."

In a couple of minutes they were sitting together. Dan got the pipe going and passed it to the old man.

"She ain't no better, grandfather."

"Takes time," said the old man, puffing. "But you got your wish. She'll be all right. You'll know when it happens. Then you won't have to come out here anymore."

Dan smoked then. "How long have you been enchanted out here, grandfather?"

"Too long."

"How come you're enchanted?"

"Don't like to talk about it," said the old man.

"Did you do something wrong?"

"Not much, I didn't think." He gazed into the bowl of the pipe. "Well, I'll tell you, son. Time was, a long time ago, I didn't use to believe in enchantments. I used to scoff and make fun of that sort of stuff, you know. Had no use for it. So this is a kind of punishment. Now I got to be enchanted for a bit, till I learn my lesson."

"Ain't you learned it yet?"

"Well, I ain't as skeptical as I used to be, I tell you that much. But tell me about yourself. Tell me about your place. You got goats? What's your main crop?"

So Dan began telling him all about the farm, and what they raised and what they did. They talked about fertilizers, and goats, and rabbits and such until the hour was up. Dan said goodbye then and slid into the water, holding the tobacco over his head.

"See you tomorrow," he called.

"See you tomorrow," the old man answered.

Diana was home when he arrived. She had been wondering why Dan had left a full cup of coffee on the table, as if he had left the house suddenly. When she saw him, she was convinced that something was strange.

"Did you fall in the stream again?" she asked.

"Huh? Oh, yeah . . . fell in the stream again," Dan said.

Diana made no comment on that, but she watched him all that evening and thought that he was acting odd, though she could not quite understand what was different about him. A couple of times she said, "Are you feeling all right, dear?"

"Sure, why not," Dan answered, and he looked at her closely. "And are *you* feeling all right, dear?"

"I'm fine, dear."

"Well, I'm fine, too."

Yet she knew something was wrong somehow.

So the next afternoon after eating, she picked up her hairbrush and told Dan she was going off to the woods. Dan said that was fine, and that he would fool around the place, maybe fix some fence. So she left and went into the woods, and Dan got his tobacco together and went out the back door.

But Diana saw him. She was hiding behind a bush to fool him because she thought something was certainly peculiar, and she was worried. How could a man fall in the stream two days in a row like that, and now what was he doing sneaking off out the back door? Diana meant to find out what the trouble was. Maybe, she thought, he has fits and falls into the water. Maybe, she thought, he is sick and needs help. Maybe he's keeping his fits a secret from me.

She came out from behind the bush when Dan was gone a ways, and she ran across to where he had walked toward the stream, following his path. It was easy to follow, for it wove right down beside the stream, and presently she could hear his voice in the distance. Carefully, slowly, she crept up near and parted some bushes to look.

And there in the middle of the stream on a pile of sticks was her husband, dripping wet, sitting next to an old gray beaver, smoking his pipe and calling the beaver "grandfather" and talking about farming.

Diana clapped both hands to her mouth. She

scuttled and crawled through the bush for several yards before she dared to let her breath out in a gasp and a wail as she moved farther off from the stream.

"Ohhhhhh . . . ohhhhhhhh, my husband is crazy. Oh, oh, I have married a crazy man, a poor crazy man. Oh, oh, what am I to do?" She curled up by a tree and moaned and held her head. "Oh, my poor crazy husband, oh, oh." Finally she remembered the chained lady and at once was hopeful. "She'll know what to do about this! Surely she'll know something to do. Maybe I can get a wish to make him well again. Quick, now, which is the way?"

And she did find the way after a bit. She broke through the bushes into the glade and ran to the little mill and swung open the door. But there inside was only an old donkey pushing around a millstone. The enchantment was over. The chained lady was free, just as she had said she'd be one day, and Diana would never

49

find her at the mill again. There was nothing left to do but sit down and cry for poor crazy Dan. Then she went home.

When Dan arrived home that afternoon, Diana was in bed. Her worry was working on her health. Dan could see she had been crying.

"I was only thinking about some things," she said to Dan. "I'm well enough." She brought his face down and kissed him. "But are you all right, dear?"

"I fell in the stream again."

"That's all right," she said, stroking his hair. "It doesn't matter."

Dan was puzzled. Now and then when she looked at him that evening, her eyes would brim up with tears. Dan wondered if that meant she was more crazy or less crazy. It seemed maybe more crazy to him, and he began doubting that his wish was helping her any. So they both worried a lot that evening, and they couldn't find much to say. And they sort of tiptoed around and kept offering to get something or do something for each other. That night they held each other tight, and each could feel the other's tears, but they said nothing.

The next morning passed quietly also. She worried about his craziness and how he had cried that night, and he worried about her craziness and her crying. They watched each other, and each thought that the other's watching was more craziness.

When they finished the midday meal, Dan sat dumbly and forgot to light his pipe. He waited for Diana to get her hairbrush and head on out to the woods. He was sad to think that his poor wife was going out to brush a donkey's mane and talk to it. But Diana would go out there no more. The chained lady was free, gone forever. Presently Dan spoke, for he was eager to talk with the old man again and tell him that his wife was getting worse.

"Aren't you going for a walk in the woods, dear?"

"No, I think not," Diana said.

"Oh. Later then, I suppose."

"No. Not later, either."

"Tomorrow, then?" asked Dan.

"Not tomorrow, either," said Diana.

Dan came up in his chair and looked closely at her, a slight hope rising in him. "But don't you want to take your hairbrush out to the woods and do something?"

"No," she said. "But of course if *you* want to go for a walk, we could go together."

And then Dan saw in his wife's eyes that she was not crazy anymore, just as the old man said it would be. Diana spoke again.

"But I suppose you'll want to go for a walk by yourself, won't you? I mean maybe you'll want to go down by the stream and have a smoke or something?"

"Not me," said Dan, because now his wish

was granted. And now there was no reason to go smoke and talk with the old man. "I guess I'll just stay around here."

"But tomorrow you'll go, won't you?"

"No, not tomorrow either. Why don't we just go for a walk together?"

And then Diana saw that *he* wasn't crazy anymore. They smiled at each other, each in a joy unknown to the other, ready to laugh or cry with relief and happiness. But just at that moment, before they could do either, a little man about five inches tall came flying up to the open window, flapping his arms like mad. There was a great earthworm slung over his shoulder, and he lit on a tree branch outside the window. For a moment he panted from the exertion of flying, then shouted in at them.

"Hey, in there! Look at me! I'm a little enchanted man. I've got to live like a bird and eat the things birds eat, and I hate it. It's a punishment. Well, never mind that. But you see this

worm I caught? They taste terrible raw, but they
ain't so bad cooked up a little. If you'll pop it
into the oven for a bit and then toss it out here,
I'll give you both a wish."

Dan and Diana looked out, but they did not
see the little man, for they did not need a wish.
They had everything they needed, everything
they could wish for. All they saw was a robin
sitting on the branch. All they could hear was
chirping.

"My," said Diana, "listen to how excited
he is."

"Almost like he's talking to us," Dan said.

"Hey!" the little man called out. "I'm a little man, not a bird. Don't you see? Don't you need a wish?" He cocked his head and shifted the great worm slung over his shoulder. "I guess not, huh? Oh well, my mistake." And he flew away with his worm.

Dan and Diana were getting set to go out to the garden just a bit later, when Diana thought about the robin again and she said, "You know, there was something strange about that bird. I've never seen a robin carry a worm over his shoulder like that before."

"Oh?" said Dan, looking down his hoe handle. "I hardly noticed."

Diana looked at him. "I just barely noticed," she said.

"In fact," said Dan, putting the hoe on his shoulder. "I didn't notice at all."

"Well, then," said Diana, "neither did I."

And out they went to hoe the garden together.